A Note from Michelle about Bunk 3, Teddy and Me

Hi! I'm Michelle Tanner. I'm nine years old. And I hate summer camp!

It's all because of this girl in my bunk named Brenda. She's *so* mean! She plays the worst tricks on me. I've been trying to get even with Brenda—but no matter what trick I play on her, she's always got a better one!

So far the only good thing about camp is all the care packages I've received from home. And that means a lot of care packages. Because I have a lot of family!

There's my dad and my two older sisters, D. J. and Stephanie. But that's not all.

My mom died when I was little. So my uncle Jesse moved in to help Dad take care of us. So did Joey Gladstone. He's my dad's friend from college. It's almost like having three dads. But that's still not all!

First Uncle Jesse got married to Becky Donaldson. Then they had twin boys, Nicky and Alex. The twins are four years old now. And they're so cute.

That's nine people. Our dog, Comet, makes ten. Sure, it gets kind of crazy sometimes. But I wouldn't change it for anything. It's so much fun to live in a full house!

FULL HOUSE™ MICHELLE novels

The Great Pet Project
The Super-Duper Sleepover Party
My Two Best Friends
Lucky, Lucky Day
The Ghost in My Closet
Ballet Surprise
Major League Trouble
My Fourth-Grade Mess
Bunk 3, Teddy and Me

Available from MINSTREL Books

For orders other than by individual consumers, Pocket Books grants a discount on the purchase of **10 or more** copies of single titles for special markets or premium use. For further details, please write to the Vice-President of Special Markets, Pocket Books, 1633 Broadway, New York, NY 10019-6785, 8th Floor.

For information on how individual consumers can place orders, please write to Mail Order Department, Simon & Schuster Inc., 200 Old Tappan Road, Old Tappan, NJ 07675.

Full House™ Michelle

Bunk 3, Teddy and Me

Cathy East Dubowski

A Parachute Press Book

Published by POCKET BOOKS
New York London Toronto Sydney Tokyo Singapore

A MINSTREL PAPERBACK *Original*

A Minstrel Book published by
POCKET BOOKS, a division of Simon & Schuster Inc.
1230 Avenue of the Americas, New York, NY 10020

A PARACHUTE PRESS BOOK

ISBN: 0-671-56834-5

First Minstrel Books printing July 1996

10 9 8 7 6 5 4 3 2 1

Cover photo by Schultz Photography

Printed in the U.S.A.

Bunk 3, Teddy and Me

Chapter 1

♡ "Please, Dad!" Michelle Tanner begged. "We have to leave now! Or I'll be the last one there!"

"Let me just double check the list, Michelle," her father said. He waved his clipboard.

Michelle sighed. She sat down on the couch next to her bags.

"Let's see," Danny Tanner said. "Sleeping bag, extra blanket, second extra blanket, towels . . . washcloths?"

Michelle nodded.

"Band-Aids, first-aid cream, sunscreen . . . bug spray?"

"Check," Michelle answered.

"Rainwear, underwear, *long* underwear—"

"Dad!" Michelle rolled her eyes.

"What?" her father asked.

"Summer camp will be over by the time we get there!"

Danny smiled. "Sorry, honey. I guess it's hard for me to let my baby go off into the woods. Better safe than sorry!"

Michelle smiled too. Her dad always said things like that. But she wished he wouldn't call her his baby. After all, she was nine years old!

Michelle was going to sleep-away camp by herself. She had gone once with her two older sisters. But this summer eighteen-year-old D.J. had a job waitressing at the Smash Club. Stephanie, Michelle's thirteen-year-old sister, was going to computer camp at her middle school.

Michelle wished one of her friends was going with her. But her best friend Cassie Wilkins had already left to spend the first month of summer at her grandmother's farm. Her other best friend, Mandy Metz, was going to Canada tomorrow with her family for summer vacation.

So Michelle was going to summer camp all by herself.

"Okay, everybody!" Danny called out. "We're leaving!"

Doors banged open all over the house. Feet stomped upstairs, downstairs—all heading toward them. The living room was suddenly packed with people!

Michelle lived in an old Victorian house with eight other people. Her dad and her two sisters. Plus Uncle Jesse, Aunt Becky, and their four-year-old twin boys, Alex and Nicky. And Joey Gladstone, her dad's best friend from college. Oh, and Comet, their golden-haired dog! It was definitely a full house!

Michelle loved them all. But at camp she would be on her own—for the first time. Nobody telling her what to think. Nobody telling her what to do.

Michelle couldn't wait!

"Just remember the most important thing," Joey said.

"What?" Michelle asked.

"Where does a skunk sleep in the woods?"

"Where?"

"Anywhere he wants to!" Joey laughed at his own joke. Joey loved to tell jokes—usually dumb ones!

"Michelle, wait!" Alex cried as he ran into the room. "You forgot Mr. Teddy!"

"For good luck!" Nicky added.

Alex stuffed the cuddly tan bear into Michelle's hands. Both boys reached up and hugged her hard. So hard Michelle almost fell down!

Everyone said good-bye. Michelle and her dad were ready to leave—finally. In the car Michelle propped up Mr. Teddy in the middle of the front seat.

Michelle loved stuffed animals. She had a huge collection. But Mr. Teddy was her favorite. He was her good-luck bear.

Good luck? Michelle thought. *Who needs*

it? I don't have to worry about that! This is going to be my best summer ever!

The skyscrapers and big-city traffic disappeared as they drove along the highway. The towns turned into woods and more woods. It seemed to Michelle as if they drove for a hundred hours through the woods! At last she spotted an old sign that said CAMP PINKWATER. FOUNDED 1923.

The car bounced as Danny turned onto the gravel road.

They passed more trees and more trees. Then Michelle cried, "There it is!"

Camp Pinkwater looked just like it did in the brochure. Only there were a lot more trees—and lots and lots of girls wandering around with their parents.

Danny and Michelle stepped up to the registration table. A tall woman with short gray hair smiled and shook Danny's hand. "How do you do? I'm Rowena Pinkwater, the camp director."

Danny smiled. "Nice to meet you. I'm

Danny Tanner. And this is my daughter Michelle. It's her first time at camp by herself. Are you sure she'll be—"

"Don't worry about a thing!" Ms. Pinkwater said cheerfully. "I treat Pinkwater girls like my own children."

She ran her pencil down a list on her clipboard. "Tanner, Tanner . . . ah, yes. You're a Bear."

"Excuse me?" Michelle said.

Ms. Pinkwater chuckled. "Each cabin is named after a woodland animal. The Bears. The Foxes. The Raccoons." She pointed with her pencil. "You will find the Bears down that path. Third cabin on the right. Pick a bunk, toss your gear. Then everybody will meet back in the mess hall at four o'clock sharp. Okay?"

Michelle nodded.

"I like Ms. Pinkwater," Danny whispered as he and Michelle walked away. "Firm but friendly."

"Uh-huh," Michelle answered. But she wasn't really listening. A group of girls walked by, and Michelle stared at them. They were wearing pink Camp Pinkwater T-shirts. They looked as if they'd been here before. And it seemed as if they had known each other forever.

Danny noticed Michelle's frown. "Don't worry, honey. You'll feel right at home as soon as you make some new friends."

"There it is, Dad." Michelle pointed as they walked down the path. "The Bears cabin."

Michelle's home-away-from-home was a wooden cabin with screened windows trimmed in green. A carved sign over the door said THE BEARS.

"Well, you brought the right stuffed animal!" Danny said. "Maybe Mr. Teddy can be your cabin's mascot."

Michelle hurried up the wooden steps. The screen door squeaked as she opened it.

Inside, three bunk beds lined the walls. Each bed had a number—one through six. Some of the beds already had gear dumped on them.

"Maybe you should take a bed by the door," Danny said.

"Why?" Michelle asked.

"On second thought, maybe *away* from the door would be better," Danny replied. "It might be drafty near the door."

"Okay," Michelle said. "But I want the top bunk!"

"Bottom's best, sweetheart," Danny assured her. "I don't want you to fall out and hit your head in the middle of the night."

Then Danny gave Michelle a big hug. It was time for him to leave. "If you get homesick—even a little—call home. Collect."

"Don't worry," Michelle said. "I *won't* get homesick."

"Well, good. Oh—here." Danny pulled a stack of postcards from his shirt pocket. They were already stamped and addressed. "Don't forget to write! Let us know how you're doing. Okay?"

Michelle smiled. "I'll write. I promise!"

Michelle waited until her dad was gone.

Then she made her first "on-my-own" decision.

She grabbed her bags and dragged them back to the bunk by the window. She threw them up onto bunk 3. *Top* bunk!

Cool! Michelle thought as she climbed up. She'd always wanted to sleep on top of a bunk bed.

Michelle looked out the screen window. She could still see her father. He grew smaller and smaller as he made his way up the hill to the car. Finally he disappeared in the crowd.

All right! Michelle pumped her fist. *I'm really on my own!*

Then something funny happened. Michelle felt a tiny little crunch of homesickness in the pit of her stomach.

She wasn't just on her own—she was all alone!

Michelle glanced around her cabin. *Well, not really alone,* she thought. *I'll be sleeping with five other girls.*

But they would all be strangers. That was

very different from being in a house with eight people—and a dog—who all loved you.

Michelle lay back on her bunk and stared at the ceiling.

I'll feel right at home as soon as I make some new friends, she told herself. *Just like Dad said.*

Screech! Bang! The screen door slammed open.

"Hey!" a mean voice shouted. "Get off my bunk!"

Chapter 2

♡ Michelle leaned over the edge of her bunk bed. "Excuse me?"

A tall, tanned girl with bright green eyes glared at her. The girl wore a Camp Pinkwater T-shirt, hiking shorts, and cool high-top sneakers. She dropped her two huge bags on the floor. Then she flipped her braid over her shoulder and jammed her fists on her hips. "That's *my* bed!"

"But it was empty!" Michelle protested. "I got here first."

"No, *I* got here first. *Last* summer," the girl said. "This was my cabin last year. Bunk 3 was my bed last year. And I want it again *this* year."

Michelle thought a moment. She sure didn't want to fight with a bunkmate on the first day of camp! And she could sort of understand why the girl wanted the same bunk as last year.

Should she just be nice and pick another bunk?

"What's your name?" Michelle asked.

"Brenda Mulroney. What's yours?"

"Michelle Tanner."

"You're new here, aren't you?"

"Yes," Michelle answered.

Brenda snorted. "Well, if you're new, you can't just move in here and try to take over. I was here before. I should have first choice."

"But that doesn't make any sense!" Michelle cried.

"Who cares?" the girl answered. "Just get off my bunk!"

Boy, this girl is mean! Michelle thought. She didn't want to start a fight. But she didn't like being bossed around, either.

Michelle remembered what Uncle Jesse

had told her once, when she had trouble with a bully at school. “You can’t let a bully push you around,” he said. “You’ve got to stand up for yourself, right from the start.”

Michelle jumped down from the top bunk.

Brenda crossed her arms and grinned. She thought she had won.

But Michelle had a surprise for Brenda. She didn’t move her things. She left them right where they were.

“Sorry, Brenda,” Michelle said in a nice but firm voice. “I was here first.”

“But—”

“I’ve got to go,” Michelle interrupted as she hurried out the screen door. “See you later!”

Michelle crunched up the gravel path. *Whew! That was hard!* But she felt good that she had stood up for herself. She could almost hear Uncle Jesse saying, *“Way to go!”*

Still, Michelle couldn’t help but worry. Would all the Bears be as grouchy as Brenda Mulroney?

* * *

Michelle joined the crowd of girls streaming along the path. They were headed toward a large wooden building. A sign in front of it said MESS HALL. Michelle knew that was camp talk for cafeteria.

A pink banner over the door said WELCOME, CAMPERS!

Inside, all the tables had been folded away and stacked against the wall. Metal chairs were lined up in rows. It looked like the auditorium at Michelle's school.

Counselors all around the room waved signs with their cabin names: THE RACCOONS, THE FOXES, THE CHIPMUNKS. Michelle spotted a pretty older girl with long blond hair. The girl was holding up a sign that said THE BEARS.

"Hi," Michelle said. "I'm a Bear. I'm Michelle Tanner."

"Hey, Michelle! I'm Donna Jones. I'm going to be your counselor." Donna spoke with a soft southern accent and had a nice smile. Michelle guessed she was about the same age as D.J.

Donna wrote *Michelle* on a name tag and held it out to her. "Bunkmates are sitting together for this meeting. Right here."

"Thanks," Michelle said. She sat down next to a tall girl with curly dark hair and a big smile.

"Hi! I'm Gina," the girl said. She pointed to the camper sitting beside her. The girl had straight chin-length brown hair and wore round wire-rimmed glasses. "This is Emily."

Emily smiled.

"Hi, I'm Michelle Tanner."

These girls seemed a lot nicer than Brenda! Michelle thought. Neither girl wore a pink Camp Pinkwater T-shirt. "Is this your first time here?" Michelle asked.

Both girls nodded.

"But don't worry," Gina said. "My cousin Andrea came here three summers ago. She told me all about it. So stick with me and you'll be fine!"

A few minutes later Brenda showed up with two other girls. They were Bears too. And they both wore Camp Pinkwater T-shirts. One had dark skin and big brown eyes. Her name tag said *Jolene.* The other wore her curly blond hair in a ponytail with a pink scrunchie. *Lisa* was written on her name tag.

Brenda glared at Michelle, then whispered something to her two friends. All three giggled as they sat down next to Emily.

"Have you met those girls?" Gina whispered.

"I sort of met the girl with the red hair," Michelle said. "Her name's Brenda." She decided not to say anything about her bunk bed fight with Brenda.

Soon the meeting started. Donna sat with the other counselors at a long table up front. Ms. Pinkwater stood up at the middle of the table.

"Welcome to Camp Pinkwater," Ms. Pinkwater announced. "To those of you who have been here before, welcome back! To those of you who are new, we hope you'll love us and come back again next year!"

Some of the girls clapped.

Ms. Pinkwater introduced all the counselors. Then she talked about the camp's history and went over the rules. She told them all about the great things they'd be doing—hiking, camping, all kinds of fun stuff. Michelle thought camp was definitely going to be fun!

Finally Ms. Pinkwater was done. "We have an hour till supper," she said. "Get to know your new bunkmates. See you back here at six."

Donna hurried over to join her campers. "Come on, Bears!" she said cheerfully. But Brenda and her friends had already jumped up and dashed outside. So Donna walked with Michelle and her new friends, Emily and Gina.

Emily smiled a lot. But she didn't talk much.

Gina talked enough for both of them! "My brothers call me Motormouth," she admitted with a laugh.

When they reached their cabin, Donna bounded up the steps. But once inside, she tripped over something on the floor.

Michelle and Emily hurried to help her up. "Are you all right?" Michelle asked.

"Thanks," Donna said, standing up. "I'm fine." Then she looked at the bags on the floor. "Whose stuff is this?"

"I think it's Michelle's," Brenda spoke up.

Michelle blinked. It *was* her stuff—scattered all over the floor!

And Brenda was sitting on a top bunk.

Bunk 3!

Michelle's bunk!

Chapter 3

"Hey!" Michelle cried. "Bunk 3 is *my* bunk!"

"I don't see your name on it," Brenda said innocently.

"But it's mine! I was—"

"Now, Michelle," Donna said. "Brenda was there first."

"But—"

"Come on, Bears," Donna said cheerfully. "Let's not argue over bunk beds. Okay? Besides," she added with a laugh. "They're *all* lumpy! How about this one, Michelle?"

Michelle frowned. Bunk 4. It was the only

one left. And it was a *bottom* bunk—right under Brenda!

What could Michelle do? She didn't want to look like a bad sport.

"Okay," Michelle said. She noticed that Jolene and Lisa had also nabbed top bunks. The new campers—Michelle, Gina, and Emily—all got stuck on the bottom.

Beep-beep! Beep-beep!

Everybody jumped.

"Don't worry!" Donna said. She held up her wrist. "It's just the beeper alarm on my watch. Ms. Pinkwater totally *hates* for anybody to be late. This is the only way I can make it anywhere on time! Well, I have to go help set up supper. See you in the mess hall at six." She winked. "Don't be late!"

The bunkmates spent the time until supper putting their things away. Michelle tacked up a picture of her family on the cabin wall. Gina chattered most of the time. And Emily listened.

"Don't you just love sleeping on the top

bunk?" Brenda asked her two friends—making sure the bottom bunkers heard her.

"Yeah—it's totally cool!" Jolene agreed.

Gina quickly plopped down on her bed, lying on her back. She raised both feet above her so they touched the bottom of Jolene's mattress. In a loud voice she said, "It's fun being on the bottom bunk too!" Then she started pushing up with her feet!

Jolene shrieked and grabbed onto her bouncing mattress.

Then Emily tried it. She gave Lisa's mattress a little bounce.

Michelle thought about it for a second. She couldn't resist! She gave Brenda a bounce too!

"No fair!" Brenda hollered. "Cut it out!"

"Don't you like the top bunk anymore?" Gina asked, laughing.

Brenda ignored her. She jumped off her bed and whispered something to Jolene and Lisa.

"Bears!" Donna called from outside.

"Supper is in ten minutes. I'll see you in the mess hall!"

Michelle sat upright to get ready for supper.

Brenda stared at Michelle in amazement. "You're not wearing *shorts,* are you?" she exclaimed.

Michelle looked down at her pink T-shirt and blue shorts. "Why not?"

Jolene and Lisa started laughing.

"Tell them, Brenda," Jolene said in between giggles.

Brenda rolled her eyes. "Everybody wears bathing suits the first night."

"Bathing suits!" Michelle exclaimed.

"No way!" Gina insisted.

"But why?" Emily asked.

"Just for fun," Jolene explained.

"It's a Camp Pinkwater tradition," Brenda added.

"Yeah," Lisa said. "Don't you guys know anything?"

"Hey, wait a minute," Gina said with a

frown. "My cousin Andrea didn't tell me anything about this tradition."

"What can I say?" Brenda shrugged. "Do what you want."

Then Brenda, Jolene, and Lisa changed into their swimsuits.

Michelle looked at Gina. "They're wearing *their* bathing suits," she whispered.

"And they've been here before," Emily added.

Gina sighed. "It must be true, then. I guess we'd better change. We don't want to look like jerks at supper!"

Michelle, Gina, and Emily changed into their bathing suits. Michelle's suit was blue with pink fish all over it. She slipped into matching blue flip-flops.

Jolene and Lisa elbowed each other and laughed when they saw Emily's bathing suit. It had tiny ducks on it and a ruffly skirt. It looked kind of babyish.

Emily blushed. "This is real old," she explained. "My mom made me bring it."

"Don't worry about it," Michelle said in a nice way. "I like it."

Gina pulled on a cherry red tank suit. Then she started digging through her stuffed backpack. "I can't find my flip-flops!" she wailed.

"We can't hang around," Brenda said. "We're going to be late." She and her two friends hurried out, giggling.

At last Gina found her flip-flops and put them on. "Thanks for waiting, guys," she said with a smile.

"What are friends for?" Michelle answered. "Besides, who wants to walk with those three?"

"I've got a bad feeling about them," Gina admitted.

"Me too," Michelle agreed.

Michelle had dreamed of Camp Pinkwater for weeks. And how she and her new bunkmates would become friends for life.

But the Bears had already split into two groups. Two groups that didn't like each other at all.

At last Michelle, Gina, and Emily hurried to the mess hall. The campgrounds were empty.

"We must really be late," Michelle said with a groan. "Come on!"

She and her friends dashed inside—and Michelle skidded to a stop.

Emily gasped.

Gina flip-flopped to a halt.

Every camper and counselor in the mess hall was staring at them.

Nobody else—*nobody!*—was wearing a bathing suit!

Not even Brenda and her buddies.

Laughter rippled across the room. Emily's face turned as red as Gina's cherry red tank suit.

"I feel like such an idiot!" Gina whispered.

"Brenda and the other two must have sneaked clothes out with them when we weren't watching!" Michelle whispered back.

Ms. Pinkwater strolled over with one eyebrow raised. She looked as if she was trying not to grin. "Going swimming, girls?" she asked. There was more laughter from the room.

Michelle tried to explain. "Brenda told us we were *supposed* to dress this way. She said it was a tradition."

"It sort of is," Donna said, coming up behind Michelle. "Every year somebody fools at least one of the new campers into wearing a bathing suit to dinner the first night."

"But why?" Emily asked.

Donna shrugged. "It's just a silly tradition—a game."

Ms. Pinkwater patted Michelle on the back. "Thanks for being such good sports about it, girls. Now run along and get your dinner."

Michelle wished they could go change. But she headed for the food line as she was told. Even though she wasn't very hungry anymore.

Even Gina was quiet as they carried their trays to an empty table.

Ms. Pinkwater looked around the mess

hall and clapped. "Okay, girls. Settle down. Now, I expect this to be the last of the pranks. Do I make myself clear?"

The campers nodded and went back to eating.

Michelle glanced at Brenda and her friends. They were pointing at Michelle, Gina, and Emily—and giggling.

Michelle looked away. She had a sinking feeling as she stared down into her plate of spaghetti that the pranks had just begun.

Chapter 4

Dear Dad,

I *hate* camp! The food is gross. The beds are hard. And this girl named Brenda is being mean to me!

First she stole my bunk. Then she made me look like a jerk in front of the whole camp.

At breakfast yesterday she and her friends put salt in the sugar bowl. Did you ever eat salty cornflakes? Yuck!

In arts and crafts we made friendship bracelets. Brenda heard me say that my favorite colors are pink and blue. So she grabbed all the pink and blue thread. I had to make a green and orange bracelet. And I hate orange!

I was a little homesick at first. But now Brenda is making everything much worse! Come get me! *Pleeeeeeese?*

Love,
Michelle

Michelle put the cap back on her pen. Then she slowly, slowly tore the letter into about fifty pieces.

She couldn't send a letter like that to her dad. She'd only been at camp two days! And she didn't want her dad to think she was a baby—that she wasn't grown up enough to go to summer camp by herself.

But it did make her feel a little better to write down her feelings.

Michelle took out one of the postcards her dad had given her. She wrote: "Camp is great! I have two new friends named Emily and Gina. Hug everybody for me. Love, Michelle."

Michelle was writing her postcard during

Read, Rest & Write. That's what Ms. Pinkwater called the hour of quiet time they had after lunch every day. They had to spend it in their cabin. They could read or nap or write letters home. They could talk to each other, but they had to be quiet. That was pretty hard for Gina!

Michelle peeked at her watch. A whole thirty minutes left. *Now what?* she thought.

Michelle reached under her bed and dragged out her backpack. She pulled out the joke book Joey had given her for a going-away present. Grinning, she lay back and began to read:

Q. Why did Shirley tiptoe into her tent?

A. Because there was a sleeping bag inside!

Q. What's the best way to make a campfire with two sticks?

A. Make sure one of the sticks is a match!

Michelle giggled. Some of the jokes were pretty corny!

Just then Donna knocked on the cabin door. "Hey, mail's here!" she called out cheerfully. She came in and put a big box down on the floor. Then she passed out letters. She gave one to Emily, Gina, Jolene, Lisa, and Michelle. But she still had a handful of letters left.

"Let's see. Another one for Michelle . . . Michelle . . . Wow, Michelle! You got five letters!"

Michelle grinned in delight as she read the return addresses. There was one from her dad. One from Alex and Nicky—probably filled with pictures they drew. They didn't know how to write yet. A letter from each of her sisters. And one from Joey—with Comet's paw print on the back!

"Anything for me?" Brenda asked Donna hopefully.

Donna bit her lip and held out empty hands. "Um, no. Sorry. Oh—wait! There's a box too. I bet *that's* yours."

Brenda smiled smugly. "Save the best for last."

Donna started to hand the box to Brenda. Then she read the label and stopped. "Oops! Sorry, Brenda. It's not for you."

"Oh." Brenda's smile disappeared. "Who's it for?"

"It's for Michelle."

"Really?" Michelle exclaimed.

Michelle caught the hurt look on Brenda's face. She felt a little sorry for her. Brenda was the only one who didn't receive anything in the mail.

"What did you get, Michelle?" Emily asked.

Michelle ripped open the box. Inside was a note from Aunt Becky: "A box of hugs from the gang at home! We miss you!"

The box was stuffed with all kinds of goodies.

Homemade cookies from Dad. Big chocolate chip cookies with M&M's! There were other treats too.

Stephanie sent the new chapter book from Michelle's favorite series. Joey sent a Magic 8 Ball—the kind that tells your fortune. There was a cassette of camp songs sung by "Jesse & Sons." Michelle giggled. Jesse was a rock singer, and he was already teaching the twins to sing harmony.

Donna chuckled. "Michelle, you hit the jackpot!"

"Need any help eating all those cookies?" Gina joked.

Michelle laughed and passed around the cookie tin. She was feeling so good. She even offered some to the "Top Bunk Trio"—Jolene, Lisa, and Brenda.

"No, thanks," Brenda mumbled without looking down from her top bunk. "I'm not hungry."

I give up, Michelle thought. There was no way she and Brenda were ever going to be friends!

That night Michelle lay in her bunk, thinking about her family. Their letters and treats made her feel really special.

Her family was so sweet!

Michelle gulped. Oh, no! Thinking about how nice her family was made her feel a little pang of homesickness! Michelle decided she could use a hug from Mr. Teddy.

She sneaked out of bed. She dug around in her pack.

Hey! Where is he? Michelle wondered. She dumped some of her stuff on the floor.

No Teddy.

Michelle turned on her flashlight so she could see better. She crouched down to look under the bed.

"Hey, Michelle!" Brenda snapped. "Turn off that flashlight. You're keeping everybody awake!"

"Michelle," Emily whispered. "Is something wrong?"

"I can't find Mr. Teddy," Michelle said.

"Hey! This is a 'girls only' cabin!" Lisa cracked.

Michelle rolled her eyes. "Mr. Teddy is my teddy bear. Has anybody seen him? He's about this big, and he's tan—"

Jolene and Lisa giggled.

"Poor baby," Jolene teased. "Can't find your teddy bear?"

"Too bad," Lisa said in baby talk. "Maybe we can buy you a bottle. Would that make you feel better?"

"No way!" Brenda put in. "No babies allowed around here!"

"I'm not a baby!" Michelle cried.

"Cut it out, guys!" Gina shouted. "I'm trying to sleep!"

"Make us!" Lisa dared her.

Crunch! Crunch! Someone was coming down the gravel path.

Michelle flicked off her flashlight and jumped in bed.

All six girls ducked under their covers.

A flashlight shone through the screen door. "What's all the noise, girls? It's after lights out." It was Ms. Pinkwater!

"Sorry, Ms. Pinkwater," Brenda said. "Michelle Tanner was talking in her sleep. It woke us all up."

What? Michelle couldn't believe it. *Oooh! That Brenda!*

The light swept over Michelle's bed. "You okay, Michelle?"

Michelle wanted to shout, "No!" Instead she answered, "Yes, Ms. Pinkwater. I'm fine."

"Good. Then let's get some sleep, girls. Morning comes pretty early around here."

Michelle waited until Ms. Pinkwater was gone. Then she sneaked out of her bed again. She pulled Gina out of her bed, and they went and sat together on Emily's bunk.

"I really want Mr. Teddy back," Michelle whispered. "Do you think Brenda could have stolen him?"

"Probably," Gina whispered. "She's mean enough to do it!"

"Why do they always have to pick on us?" Emily complained.

"Let's pay them back!" Gina declared. "I've got an idea."

Gina moved even closer to Michelle and Emily. "We'll start playing pranks *on them,*" she whispered. "I know tons of pranks."

"Hey!" Brenda hissed down from her top bunk. "What are you guys whispering about?"

"Nothing!" Michelle whispered back.

"Michelle's just talking in her sleep again!" Gina joked.

Before they went back to their bunks, Michelle and her friends promised to stick together—to play some great pranks on Brenda and her friends, and to find Mr. Teddy.

They sealed their promise with a secret three-handed Bottom Bunkers' handshake.

The bunk wars were on.

Chapter 5

The next morning Michelle and her two friends woke up before their bunkmates.

"P-U!" Gina whispered, holding her nose.

"Shhh!" Michelle whispered, trying not to giggle. "Do you want to wake everybody up and ruin our first trick?"

They had gathered up the top bunkers' sneakers. Now they were tying the shoelaces of all six sneakers together. Gina even showed them how to tie some really good double knots!

Then the three girls sneaked off to the mess hall.

Brenda and her friends showed up *really*

late for breakfast. They were wearing their sneakers, but they looked mad. Especially since all the blueberry waffles were gone!

Ms. Pinkwater didn't give them a chance to explain. Instead she lectured them about the importance of being on time.

At the end of breakfast Brenda stopped by Michelle's table. Brenda was smiling. But her words were far from sweet.

"This means war, Michelle! This means war!"

That afternoon the girls in Michelle's cabin had archery class. Michelle felt like Robin Hood as she aimed the bow and arrow at the bull's-eye on the round target.

But every time she or Gina or Emily shot, Brenda and her friends coughed really loud. Or waved their arms and jumped up and down. Or faked sneezing, "Ah-CHOO!"

Michelle couldn't concentrate. She missed the target every time.

So when it was Brenda's turn, Gina shouted, *"Miss it!"*

"Okay, Gina. Back to your cabin," announced Anita, the counselor who taught archery. "That's not the way to behave."

"But . . . but . . ." Gina tried to explain. Brenda just grinned.

That night Emily slid into bed—and screamed! *Someone* had planted a fake snake under her covers.

The next morning Brenda went to the bathroom. This time it was her turn to scream. *Somebody* had squeezed toothpaste all over the toilet seat!

At morning swim in the lake Brenda sneaked up on Michelle on the dock and dropped cold wet sand down her bathing suit. Michelle yelled so loud, all the counselors hurried over to her.

"It's nothing," Michelle admitted, hopping from one foot to another as the cold sand settled down into the bottom of her suit.

Michelle watched Brenda swim over to Jolene and Lisa and some other girls Michelle didn't know on the diving platform. She tried not to think about Brenda. But she couldn't help worrying—maybe Gina's pranks weren't such a good idea after all.

No matter what they did, Brenda seemed to do something worse. And they still hadn't found Mr. Teddy.

Maybe we should all try to make up, Michelle thought. *We'll try to be friends. And I'll just ask Brenda to give Mr. Teddy back.*

Michelle thought about it on her way back to her bunk that afternoon. *Yes, that's what we should do,* she decided—until she went inside and found the note on her bunk.

She read it and gasped. "It's a ransom note!" she cried.

Gina and Emily hurried over. Brenda and her friends weren't there. So Michelle read it out loud: " 'Help me, Michelle! I'm hungry! Please come and get me! Love, Mr. Teddy.' "

"That's so mean!" Emily cried. "Who could have done it?"

Gina rolled her eyes. "Do you have to ask? Brenda and her creepy friends, of course."

"Wait!" Michelle added. "There's more.

'Take your goody box from home to Haunted Hollow—tonight. Leave it next to the Hanging Tree. Tomorrow go back to the Hanging Tree at midnight. Mr. Teddy will be there. And don't tell anyone—or Mr. Teddy gets the stuffing knocked out of him!'

"I can't believe it!" Michelle cried. She had never felt so angry! She stormed out of the cabin with Gina and Emily marching right behind her. They tracked down Brenda, playing tetherball with some other campers.

Michelle poked Brenda in the back. "Give me back Mr. Teddy!" she shouted.

Some of the other girls giggled.

Brenda turned around and smirked. "Get a life, Michelle."

"Brenda!" Michelle cried. "If you don't—"

"Girls!" Ms. Pinkwater shouted from across the yard. "Is everything okay?"

"Yes, Ms. Pinkwater," Brenda called out with a big fake smile. She held up the ball. "Your turn, Michelle."

Michelle didn't want to get in trouble with Ms. Pinkwater. So she took the ball—and whacked it *hard!*

She couldn't prove Brenda had stolen her teddy bear. And Brenda wouldn't admit it. What was she going to do?

She loved Mr. Teddy. She had to save him.

But she definitely did not want to go out in the middle of the night—to a place called Haunted Hollow.

Chapter 6

That night Michelle waited in bed until the camp was dark and quiet. She crossed her fingers. Then she got up and pulled her goody box out from under her bed. She looked at Gina and Emily. They had fallen asleep. Brenda, Jolene, and Lisa were asleep too—or maybe they were *pretending* to be asleep!

Michelle quietly tiptoed out the door and down the steps.

A full moon lighted her way. But it was still really spooky.

Haunted Hollow was a Camp Pinkwater legend. Donna had told them all about it. It was a place in the woods that ghosts haunted, everyone said. A place where a big, creepy tree stood—called the Hanging Tree.

Donna said it was just a story, something fun to tell around a campfire. But Michelle shivered anyway. She didn't want to think about it!

"Michelle!" someone whispered.

She whirled around.

It was Gina in her jammies. Beside her Emily shivered in her shortie nightgown in the cool night air.

"We can't let you go to Haunted Hollow by yourself!" Gina said. "We're coming too."

"Thanks!" Michelle cried. "You two are the best!"

Together the three girls stumbled through the darkness. The path to Haunted Hollow was long and winding and scary in the dark. But they didn't want to use their flashlights. Someone might see them—someone like Ms. Pinkwater. Then they'd be in big trouble.

At last they came to a clearing in the

woods. A twisted tree reached up toward the moon like a bony hand. The Hanging Tree!

Michelle's hands shook as she laid the goody box on the ground next to the tree. Then the three girls ducked behind some bushes. They were scared. But they wanted to see who came for the box.

It's got to be Brenda! Michelle thought.

The girls waited and waited.

An owl hooted.

But no one came.

Michelle yawned.

"This is silly," Gina said finally, standing up. "Nobody's going to come as long as we're here. Let's go back."

Michelle sighed. "I guess you're right."

The girls hurried back to their cabin. Brenda and her friends were still asleep in their bunks.

Michelle stared at Brenda. Could she be telling the truth? Maybe she really wasn't Mr. Teddy's kidnapper.

Michelle had to find out. And as she fell asleep, she came up with a plan.

* * *

Michelle's plan was simple. The next day she and Gina and Emily would spend the entire day following their bunkmates. But it was harder than they expected—because for once the girls split up!

Michelle shadowed Brenda. Gina tailed Jolene. And Emily stuck to Lisa like a pesky kid sister.

Sooner or later one of the terrible threesome would have to go to Haunted Hollow. Michelle was sure of it.

Michelle was so busy watching Brenda during an afternoon softball game, she struck out twice—and missed a fly ball!

Gina paddled a canoe around the lake, following Jolene. But just as she finally caught up to Jolene, her canoe tipped. Gina was soaking wet!

Emily saddled up and went horseback riding for the first time to keep an eye on Lisa. Boy, was Emily's rear end sore that night!

But none of the girls headed for the Hanging Tree the entire day. "I don't get it," Michelle told her friends at supper. "There's no way any of them could have slipped off to Haunted Hollow today without us noticing."

"Maybe they plan to wait till it gets dark," Gina suggested. "It's easier not to get caught."

"Then we can't let them out of our sight for a minute," Michelle said.

The rest of the evening dragged by. Michelle thought she'd go crazy waiting. Even a movie in the mess hall—*King Kong*—couldn't take her mind off Mr. Teddy. She hoped he was okay.

Michelle and her friends sat right behind their suspects during the movie. They might try to sneak off in the dark!

But Brenda didn't budge. She just gobbled up a ton of popcorn and watched the movie with Lisa and Jolene.

At last it was lights out. Michelle was sleepy. But a few minutes before midnight she slipped out of bed. She woke up Gina and Emily.

If Brenda didn't take Mr. Teddy, Michelle wanted to find out who did. Together the three girls sneaked off to Haunted Hollow for the second time.

Clouds drifted across the moon. It was chilly and hard to see. Michelle's teeth chattered as she led her friends to the Hanging Tree.

"Look!" Michelle cried. "It's gone!"

Sure enough, the goody box was nowhere to be seen.

In its place sat a shopping bag.

Michelle peered inside.

She pulled out something big and furry.

Was it . . . Mr. Teddy?

Michelle clicked on her flashlight—and gasped.

It was a huge furry pink bedroom slipper!

"We were tricked!" Michelle cried. "That Brenda! Just wait—"

"Michelle!" A flashlight blinded her for a moment.

"Uh, hi, Donna," Gina mumbled.

"What are you girls doing out here?" Donna asked. It was the first time they'd seen her without a smile on her face.

Emily's mouth opened, but nothing came out.

Gina grabbed Michelle by the shoulders and shook her. "Michelle was . . . sleep-walking!" she explained to their counselor. "Emily and I had to chase her and bring her back."

"Sleepwalking with a shopping bag?" Donna asked.

"She was dreaming about shopping—right, Michelle?"

"Uh—right." Michelle smiled shakily.

"Well, get back to bed." Donna shook her head. "Don't wake the other girls—and no more sleepwalking!"

Without a word they followed Donna back to the cabin.

Michelle couldn't believe what she saw inside. Brenda, Jolene, and Lisa—sound asleep.

How could Brenda be the kidnapper? It just didn't seem possible.

Michelle was exhausted. She crawled into bed and pulled the covers over her head.

She felt rotten. She'd given away her whole box of goodies. And she still hadn't gotten Mr. Teddy back. *I'm sorry I let you down!* she whispered into the darkness to her missing teddy bear.

It looked as if Mr. Teddy's good luck had run out.

She just hoped Mr. Teddy was still in one piece!

Wherever he was. . . .

Chapter 7

Michelle felt rotten all day the next day. A letter from home didn't help much.

"Dear Michelle," her dad wrote. "Glad to hear you're having so much fun at camp. . . ."

Yeah, right, Michelle thought.

But she had to laugh out loud at the letter she received from Cassie. She'd sent a picture of her taken at her grandmother's farm—milking a cow!

She showed it to her friends as they walked back to their cabin.

Gina loved it. "I think I'll go to farm camp next summer," she joked.

Just then they spotted Brenda hanging out with Jolene and Lisa on the steps of the Raccoons' cabin. One of the Raccoons had curly blond hair just like Lisa.

Michelle started to walk right past them.

But then she heard Brenda say, "Hey, Jolene—do you want another cookie?"

Michelle glanced sideways. Brenda was passing around a large plastic bag of cookies. Big cookies. Cookies with M&M's!

"Dad's cookies!" Michelle gasped.

"What?" Gina asked.

Michelle pointed at Brenda. "Look!"

"All right!" Gina grinned. "We've caught her—red-handed!"

Michelle rushed over to Brenda and her friends.

"Hi, Michelle," Brenda said, pretending to be friendly. "Do you know Lisa's sister, Charlene? And this is Alina. They're both Raccoons."

Michelle didn't even smile. "Give me back my cookies!" she demanded. "And Mr. Teddy!"

"Yeah," Gina added. "And all the other stuff, too!"

Brenda looked puzzled. "What are you talking about?"

"Those are my cookies—from my goody box. The ones my dad sent me. I left the box by the Hanging Tree—just like you told me. *You're* Mr. Teddy's kidnapper!"

Brenda stared at Michelle as if she were crazy. Her friends poked each other and giggled.

"Your dad is not the only one who knows how to bake cookies, Michelle," Brenda said. "My mother sent me these."

Michelle paused. Brenda had a point. Michelle couldn't prove those were her cookies.

"I give up," Michelle muttered. "Come on, Gina." They started to walk away.

"Maybe some *bears* ate *your* cookies," Brenda said.

"Or," Charlene added, "maybe some *raccoons.*"

Oh, I get it, Michelle thought. Brenda didn't pick up the goody box from the

Haunted Hollow. She had Alina and Charlene do it!

Michelle stomped over to Brenda. "Give me back my stuff—or else!" she demanded.

Brenda stood up and faced Michelle, nose to nose. "Or else what?"

"Or else—or else I'll make you!" Michelle shouted.

"Okay, Michelle," Brenda yelled back. "Make me."

"Girls!" a voice rang out. "What's going on!"

Michelle froze.

The crowd parted as Ms. Pinkwater marched up.

"Brenda! Michelle!" Ms. Pinkwater's voice was low but firm. "In my office. Now."

Ms. Pinkwater sat behind her big oak desk and stared at the girls. "This is not the kind of behavior I expect at Camp Pinkwater."

"Camp *Stink*water!" Michelle heard Brenda mumble.

"What's that, Brenda?" Ms. Pinkwater asked.

"Nothing . . ." Brenda replied.

Ms. Pinkwater stared thoughtfully at Michelle. Her eyes turned to Brenda. Then a half smile played across her lips.

"I sense that I have a problem here between you two," the director said. "And I'm going to fix it."

"How?" Michelle asked nervously.

"Well, you know the whole camp is going on an overnight hike to Highland Lake on Saturday," Ms. Pinkwater began. "Every girl will be paired up with one other girl. Pinkwater Pals, I call them. Each pair will hike together, do projects together, sleep together in a small tent. It's a way for you girls to learn how to get along together."

Uh-oh. Michelle had a really bad feeling about this. Ms. Pinkwater wouldn't . . . she couldn't . . .

"Michelle and Brenda—you two will be Pinkwater Pals. By the end of the trip I expect you two to have worked out your differences. *And* be the best of friends."

Brenda snorted. "Yeah, right. In a million years."

Exactly! Michelle thought.

"What's that, Brenda?" Ms. Pinkwater asked again.

"Nothing . . ." Brenda muttered. But she shot Michelle a look that said, *This will be the worst overnight hike of your life!*

Chapter 8

Fweeeeet!

Ms. Pinkwater's whistle scattered birds in the early morning air. "Okay, girls! Line up with your Pinkwater Pal. If anybody needs the bathroom, you've got three minutes! Let's get ready to move. It's a long hike to Highland Lake."

The campers stood in groups along one of the gravel paths. "Well, here we go," Michelle said gloomily to her two friends. She was about to pair up with Brenda for the day.

"Don't worry," Emily said. "We'll be right behind you."

"That Brenda better watch her step," Gina added. She wagged her finger at Michelle. "Don't let her push you around, okay?"

Michelle smiled at her two friends. "Thanks, guys!"

The sun shone brightly as they hiked through the woods. It was a beautiful day.

Michelle felt as if she should be having fun.

But it's no fun being stuck with Brenda! Michelle thought.

Brenda and Michelle walked side by side. They didn't say a word to each other. Every now and then Brenda would turn and make a mean face at Michelle.

Just ignore her, Michelle told herself.

Slowly Michelle began to enjoy the hike. She loved being outdoors.

Gina made everyone laugh with a marching chant she learned from one of her brothers.

Then Ms. Pinkwater stopped to point out a waterfall in the distance. As they watched quietly, a deer and her fawn stopped to drink.

"It's beautiful," Brenda murmured in amazement.

"Yeah," Michelle agreed.

Suddenly both girls glared at each other. They'd forgotten that they weren't speaking!

They marched on until lunchtime—when they stopped by a cool, clear stream. The sun had grown hot. Michelle, Emily, and Gina peeled off their shoes and socks. They sat on a rock and dangled their feet in the water. Several other campers waded up to their knees.

Brenda's friends sat down near her and Michelle. Brenda had a funny look on her face. "Hey, Michelle," she said, trying to sound friendly.

"What?"

"I've been thinking." Brenda splashed her toes in the water. "This is no fun. Let's forget everything and be pals, okay?" Brenda stuck out her hand to shake.

"Huh?" Michelle was surprised. Could Brenda really be tired of fighting?

Michelle started to put out her hand.

Then she jerked it back. She remembered a practical joke that Joey once played on Stephanie. He had a hand buzzer in his hand. When he shook Stephanie's hand, she got buzzed with a weird shock.

"Open your hand," Michelle demanded.

Brenda looked surprised. She opened her hand and turned it palm up. It was empty.

"Okay . . ." Michelle said slowly. Maybe this was for real. Maybe Brenda would finally give her back Mr. Teddy. She shook hands. It was a normal handshake.

Brenda grinned. So did Lisa and Jolene.

"Let's each lunch!" Gina announced. "I'm starving!"

"So am I!" Michelle agreed. She dug into her backpack for her bag lunch. Everyone had the same food—a sandwich, an apple, some chips, and a juice box.

Michelle unwrapped her sandwich and started to take a bite.

"Ooops!" Jolene bumped into Michelle—*hard.*

Michelle's sandwich flew out of her hands.

"Oh, *no!*" she cried.

Plop!

Right into the stream! Michelle's stomach rumbled again as she watched her sandwich slowly sink. "I hope the fish like peanut butter," she said with a sigh.

"Oh, Michelle!" Jolene squealed. "I'm so sorry!"

"That's *terrible!*" Brenda said. She pulled a sandwich from her pack and held it out. "Here. I'm not that hungry. You can have mine."

"Really?" Michelle asked.

"Sure—take it."

Why is Brenda being so nice? Michelle wondered. Maybe her bunkmate wasn't that bad after all. Maybe she really was tired of fighting.

Michelle looked at Brenda's sandwich. She *was* pretty hungry.

"Thanks," Michelle said, unwrapping the

sandwich. "We'll share," she added. She handed half the sandwich back to Brenda. Then she took a bite.

"Bleccch!" Michelle screeched, spitting it out. Something tasted awful! Her tongue was on fire!

Michelle grabbed her canteen of water and rinsed her mouth. "Ugh! What kind of sandwich was *that?"*

Michelle lifted the top of her sandwich to take a look and gasped. Somebody had sprinkled the peanut butter sandwich with pepper. Tons and tons of pepper!

"Gotcha!" Brenda cried. She took her real sandwich out of her lunch bag and began to eat.

The whole thing was a setup. It was so mean! Michelle couldn't believe it.

"You're a creep, Brenda!" Gina shouted.

Michelle was angry. She couldn't believe she'd fallen for such a rotten trick. What a fool she'd been for thinking Brenda could be nice.

"Ooooh," Gina growled. "Brenda's really the worst!"

"Michelle, you can have half my sandwich," Emily offered. "But let's go eat somewhere else."

"Fine," Michelle agreed. "But promise me you'll never let me forget."

"Forget what?"

Michelle glared over her shoulder at Brenda. "The first rule of camp war. *Never* trust the enemy!"

Chapter 9

"I found the pine cone," Michelle said. "Did you collect three types of leaves?"

"Uh-huh," Brenda answered, nodding.

Michelle didn't trust Brenda. But she did have to talk to her. How else could the two Pink-water Pals finish their nature scavenger hunt?

Michelle glanced at her watch. If they didn't hurry, they were going to miss out on all the prizes!

"Quick! What's left on the list?" Michelle asked.

Brenda studied the words. A funny look passed over her face. "Do we have to get *everything?*"

"I'm pretty sure we're supposed to," Michelle said.

"What if we can't find something?" Brenda argued. "What if—"

"We're wasting time!" Michelle said. She grabbed the list from Brenda's hand. "What don't we have?"

"Hey—give that back!" Brenda shouted.

"The list doesn't belong to you, Brenda," Michelle reminded her. "We're supposed to be partners, remember?" She handed Brenda the brown paper bag full of the stuff they had collected. Then she glanced down at the list. It looked as if everything had been checked off.

No, wait. One more item was left.

A worm.

"Yuck," Michelle muttered. "Maybe we can find one under a rock or something."

Michelle found a small rock and turned it over. A handful of startled bugs scurried into the grass. But no worms.

Michelle glanced back at Brenda. Brenda hadn't moved an inch.

"Are you going to help me look?" Michelle asked.

Brenda didn't answer, but she followed Michelle.

Michelle used a fat stick to shove a thick layer of leaves aside. "Hey, I found some! Quick! Help me catch one!"

Brenda backed away.

Michelle shook her head. She'd just have to grab one herself. *But how do you catch a worm?* she asked herself. She wrinkled her nose. *I sure don't want to touch it!*

"I know!" Michelle said out loud. She dug in her backpack. She wanted to find the metal camp cup Aunt Becky had loaned her from her old Girl Scout days. Michelle pulled out the cup and began using it as a shovel to scoop up the worms.

"I got two!" Michelle exclaimed proudly. "Brenda! Quick! Bring me the bag!"

But instead of walking toward her, Brenda backed away.

"Brenda!" Michelle hurried over. "Hold out the bag!"

Brenda was staring at the cup of worms as if it were filled with poison. Her hand trembled as she held out the bag.

Michelle tried to shake the worms into the bag.

"Aaaaagghh!" Brenda dropped the bag and ran.

All their treasures scattered on the ground. And the worms were wiggling away!

Michelle took a deep breath. She picked up one of the worms with two fingers and quickly dropped it into the sandwich bag.

"Gross!" she said with a shiver. But it wasn't really that bad. The worm felt like a fat piece of wiggling spaghetti.

Michelle put everything back in the grocery bag and stood up. "Brenda? Brenda, where are you?"

She spotted Brenda a few yards down the trail—sitting on a rock, trembling. She had her arms wrapped around her.

Michelle ran down the trail. "What's wrong? Are you okay?"

"D-don't you dare tell anybody!" Brenda whispered.

"Huh? Tell who what?" Michelle asked.

"About the worms . . ."

Michelle blinked. "What about the worms?"

Brenda shrugged.

"You mean—you're scared of worms?"

Brenda bit her lip and nodded. "Somebody put a whole bunch of them down the back of my shirt once. It was"—Brenda shuddered—"awful!"

Michelle almost started to feel sorry for her.

But Brenda's face suddenly twisted into a scowl. "Listen, Michelle. If you tell anybody, you're dead meat! Got it?" Then she grabbed the list and stomped off toward the group.

Michelle and Brenda were the last ones to rejoin the group. Everyone else had finished the scavenger hunt ahead of them.

Gina and Emily rushed over to Michelle.

"We came in second!" Emily gushed.

"Look what we won!" Gina said. They held up pink Camp Pinkwater sweatshirts.

Michelle wished she could have been on their team.

Then Ms. Pinkwater announced, "Good job, girls! We'll take a twenty-minute snack break. Just don't wander off. We still have another thirty-minute hike to our overnight campsite."

The counselors handed out granola bars.

"What's up?" Emily asked Michelle.

"What do you mean?" Michelle said as she took a bite.

"Come on! You've got a funny look on your face," Gina said. "And Brenda looks weird. What happened between you two?"

Michelle bit her lip. She thought about the words her father always told her: If you don't have something nice to say, don't say anything.

But Brenda is so horrible, Michelle thought. *And Dad's not here!*

"Guess what I found out?" Michelle told her friends.

"What?" Emily and Gina exclaimed together.

"Guess what big bad Brenda is scared of?"

"What?"

"Worms!" Michelle whispered.

Emily wrinkled her nose under her glasses. "I don't like worms much either."

"Neither do I," Michelle said. "But Brenda doesn't just think they're icky. She's *really* afraid of them! She says somebody put some down her shirt once. I asked her to hold a sandwich bag while I put two worms in it. She screamed and ran away."

Gina and Emily giggled.

"Hey," Gina said. "I've got a great idea! We can get back at Brenda for that sandwich trick she played on you."

"How?" Michelle asked.

Gina put her arms around Michelle's and Emily's shoulders. "Tonight at the campfire we'll offer Brenda some gorp."

"What's gorp?" Emily asked.

"It's a snack hikers eat on the trail for

energy," Michelle explained. "My sister D.J. told me it stands for 'Good Old Raisins and Peanuts.' Get it? G-O-R-P. Gorp! Sometimes people put other things in the mix too. Like M&M's."

"Mmmm! Sounds good," Emily said. "But why do we want to give some to Brenda?"

"It won't really be gorp!" Gina explained. "She'll stick her hand in a can, *expecting* gorp. But she'll grab a handful of worms instead! Get it?"

"Gross!" Michelle said.

"That's awful!" Emily agreed.

Still, they couldn't help but giggle.

"How about it?" Gina pressed.

"I don't know." Emily looked worried. "Will this get us in trouble?"

"Don't worry!" Gina insisted. "Brenda's sneaky with her pranks. We can be sneaky too. We'll get Brenda when Ms. Pinkwater's not looking. Come on! It's our chance to *really* get back at her. Michelle, it might even make her leave you alone for good!"

"That *would* be nice," Michelle agreed.

She thought about losing bunk 3 to Brenda the first day—and being tricked into wearing bathing suits to dinner. She thought about the pepper sandwich.

And she thought about losing Mr. Teddy and paying the ransom and still not getting him back. She wondered where he was. Now she was sure Brenda knew!

"Let's do it," Michelle said at last. She and her friends slapped each other high fives. "I can't wait to see Brenda squirm like a worm. She deserves it!"

Chapter 10

♡ At supper all the campers sat with their Pinkwater Pals. Michelle sat next to Brenda. Emily and Gina sat to her left. Brenda's friends sat on the other side of Brenda.

"Psst! Michelle!" Gina unzipped her backpack a little.

Michelle spotted a coffee can inside.

"All set!" Gina said gleefully.

Emily looked worried. "Are you *sure* you want to go through with this, Michelle?"

Michelle felt a small prickle of doubt.

"Hey, Michelle!" Lisa shouted over at her. "Want some of Brenda's sloppy joe?"

"It's her own special recipe!" Jolene joked.

Michelle turned back to Emily. "I'm sure!"

After supper a few counselors and campers headed to the stream to wash the dishes. Donna went to find another big log for the fire. And Ms. Pinkwater had to put some calamine lotion on an itchy camper.

"Michelle! Quick!" Gina whispered. "Now's our chance!" She pulled the coffee can out of her pack. "Do you want to do it?"

Michelle thought about the worms.

"Quick!" Gina said. "We don't have much time!"

"Okay, okay," Michelle agreed, even though she didn't really want to do it anymore. She grabbed the can. "Want some gorp?" she asked Brenda.

Brenda pretended to gag. "Not if *you* guys made it."

"I want some!" Jolene squealed. "Gimme!"

Uh-oh! Michelle thought. *Now what?* She

couldn't let Jolene put her hand in the can. That would ruin the joke on Brenda.

"Wait!" Gina suddenly cried. "Give me the gorp, Michelle. We don't want to share with Brenda. She'll get her germs in it. Then we'll all get sick and die!"

Sure enough—Gina made Brenda mad! Brenda jumped up. "Give me some of that!" she insisted.

Gina pulled off the lid. She pranced around with the can held high over her head. "You can't have any!"

Brenda grabbed the can. She and Gina wrestled over it.

Then Gina smiled and let go—just as Brenda yanked.

Eeeeeewwwww!"

The can flipped in the air. Brenda was showered with worms! Worms in her hair, on her arms, all over her clothes—everywhere! Brenda shrieked.

Around the campfire girls shouted and screamed. They pointed at Brenda, laughing their heads off. Michelle and Gina laughed too. It was so gross and funny and awful! Even Emily was giggling.

Only one person didn't laugh.

Brenda.

"I hate you!" she cried. "I hate you all!"

Then she ran to her tent as she burst into tears!

Chapter 11

Michelle should have felt great.

Wasn't this what she wanted? To get back at Brenda? To make Brenda feel as bad as she'd made Michelle feel?

But Michelle didn't feel great. She felt *rotten.*

She hadn't expected Brenda to cry. Not big, tough Brenda.

It felt rotten to make somebody cry.

Michelle looked around the campfire. A lot of the girls were still laughing or whispering. Even Brenda's so-called friends—Lisa and Jolene—were cracking up about the worms.

Michelle knew what it felt like to be laughed at. To feel stupid in front of a whole bunch of kids.

Michelle jumped up. "We shouldn't have done that to Brenda," she told the other campers. "We shouldn't have laughed."

"Michelle!" Gina yanked on her arm, trying to make her sit down.

"Aw, what's the big deal?" a girl with short black hair called out across the fire. "It was funny!"

"It was *mean,*" Michelle answered. "I'm going to go tell Brenda I'm sorry."

Gina's mouth hung open in shock.

But Emily was smiling. "You want me to go with you?" she asked quietly.

"No," Michelle answered. "I'll go by myself."

Michelle hurried to the tent she was supposed to share with Brenda. She stopped just outside it. She could see the soft glow from a flashlight inside.

"Knock, knock!" Michelle called out. She

tapped on the side of the tent and stuck her head inside.

Brenda's head snapped around. Michelle saw her hide something behind her back.

"Hi, Brenda," Michelle said.

"Get out of here!" Brenda shot back.

Michelle frowned. "I want to talk to you. I want to—"

"Don't you understand English? Leave me alone!"

"I'm trying to be nice!" Michelle replied.

"Yeah, right," Brenda said. "Nice *stinks.* And so do you!"

Chapter 12

Michelle sat down next to Brenda. "I'm sorry," Michelle said. "It's just that I was so mad at you today! All I wanted to do was get back at you. I thought it would make me feel good to make you feel bad. But it just made me feel worse."

"Is this a joke?" Brenda asked.

"No!" Michelle exclaimed. "That's what I'm trying to say! I'm sick of all these jokes. I'm sorry I hurt your feelings."

Brenda didn't say anything for a moment. Then she sighed and pulled a silvery picture frame from behind her back. In it was a photograph of a smiling couple. The woman had green eyes and hair the same color as Brenda's.

"Is that your mom and dad?" Michelle asked.

Brenda nodded sadly. "She died when I was four."

"I'm sorry," Michelle said softly. "My mom died when I was little too. But I don't really remember her."

"My mom was the best," Brenda went on. She swiped at her right eye. "Since then it's been just me and my dad—till now."

"Did something happen to your dad too?"

"Yes!" Brenda said. "He got married again! And now there are these two other kids living in *our* house. Bossing me around—trying to take over. Dad says they're just trying to be *nice.* Well, I say *nice* stinks."

"Are the two kids boys or girls?" Michelle asked.

"Boys!" Brenda exclaimed. "They pick on me all the time. And I got kicked out of my room because it was the biggest—big enough for those two. I had to move into the *guest* room. In my own house!"

"Are your stepbrothers the ones who put worms down your shirt?" Michelle guessed.

"Yeah. And you know what's even worse?" Brenda exclaimed. "My stepmother is expecting a new baby in September. Then they'll probably move me out to the back porch!"

Michelle giggled. But Brenda looked as if she was going to cry again. "That's the real reason my dad got rid of me!"

"What do you mean?" Michelle exclaimed.

Brenda's words tumbled out. "Dad doesn't love me as much as his *new* family. So he shipped me off to Camp Stinkwater. I didn't even want to come this year."

Michelle thought about her own father. Sometimes he got really mad at her. But she always knew he loved her. "Is your dad nice?" Michelle asked.

"He's the best dad in the whole world!" Brenda exclaimed.

Michelle grinned. "Then he couldn't really stop loving you—just like that, could he?"

"It feels like it," Brenda said.

"I've got a huge family too," Michelle said. "There's always so much going on. Sometimes people forget to be nice to each other. Then I have to remind them."

Brenda seemed to think about that.

"And then my nephews Nicky and Alex were born," Michelle added. "They were all anybody could think about. I was jealous at first. But I got over it. Babies are like puppies. Everybody goes nuts over them—no matter who they are!"

Brenda giggled. "Well, I do like puppies."

"Hey, Gina has three older brothers," Michelle said. "She even likes them! Maybe she could give you some tips on how to handle your new brothers."

"Do you think she would?" Brenda asked. She glanced down. "I haven't been very nice."

"None of us has," Michelle admitted.

"But—I guess it's kind of hard to be nice when you feel terrible."

Brenda smiled—a real smile. Then she dug into her pack and pulled out something tan and furry.

"Here," she said. "I'm releasing the hostage."

"Mr. Teddy!" Michelle squealed, hugging her old bear. He was all right. He still had all his stuffing!

"I was going to roast him with the marshmallows," Brenda joked. "But . . . I changed my mind."

"But how did you do it?" Michelle sputtered. "We followed you guys around. You never left the camp."

"You know Lisa's sister, Charlene? In the Raccoons? She and her friend Alina helped us pull off the, uh, bear-napping. They hid the bear for us. And they picked up the goody box at the Hanging Tree."

Somehow Michelle couldn't be mad at Brenda anymore. Especially now that she had Mr. Teddy back safe and sound.

Michelle stuck out her hand. "Want to end the war?"

"Yeah." Brenda grinned and shook Michelle's hand.

"I'll make you a promise," Brenda said. "When we get back to the cabin, you can have bunk 3 if you want. It will make our truce official."

"All right!" Michelle smiled. The second week of camp promised to be a whole lot more fun than the first!

"I hope everything works out for you," Michelle told Brenda. "Hey! Maybe the new baby will be a girl! Sisters are great. I have two of them!"

Brenda laughed.

Michelle laughed too.

The bunk wars were officially over!

Michelle gave Mr. Teddy a big hug. He really was her good-luck bear!

For information about
Mary-Kate + Ashley's Fun Club™,
the Olsen Twins' only
official fan club, write to:

Mary-Kate + Ashley's Fun Club™
859 Hollywood Way, Suite 412
Burbank, California 91505